The Beeman

Written by Jill Eggleton
Illustrated by Jim Storey

Rigby

The beeman
takes care of bees.
He likes bees.
Bees are in his garden
and bees are in his house.

3

On Saturday,
the beeman looked
in his book.

"Good!" he said.
"No work today.
I am staying home."

Beeman's Diary

But the phone rang
and rang and rang.

The beeman went
to get the bees.

"Bees, bees," he said.
"Come with me."

The bees went
to the beeman's house.
The beeman looked
at the bees.
"The bees are happy,"
he said.

The beeman sat
in his chair and
he went to sleep.

But the phone rang.

"I'm **not** coming,"
said the beeman.
"You will have to wait
until tomorrow!"

A Diary

Monday

- Make a bee house.

- Go to the bee store.

Tuesday

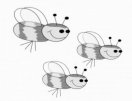

Guide Notes

Title: The Beeman
Stage: Early (2) – Yellow

Genre: Fiction
Approach: Guided Reading
Processes: Thinking Critically, Exploring Language, Processing Information
Written and Visual Focus: Diary, Speech Bubbles
Word Count: 148

THINKING CRITICALLY
(sample questions)
- What do you think this story could be about?
- Focus on the title and discuss. Ask: "What do you think might be special about this man?"
- Why do you think the beeman wanted to stay home?
- Why do you think the bees went with the beeman?
- Why do you think the beeman told the man at the end of the story that he should wait until tomorrow?

EXPLORING LANGUAGE

Terminology
Title, cover, illustrations, author, illustrator

Vocabulary
Interest words: garden, Saturday, happy, chair, work, rang, phone, tomorrow
High-frequency words (reinforced): the, in, looks, he, not, likes, are, his, on, am, I, good, no, me, help, and, my, like, to, get, said, went, home, with, come, you
Compound word: beeman
Positional word: in

Print Conventions
Capital letter for sentence beginnings and names (**B**eeman, **S**aturday), periods, quotation marks, commas, exclamation marks